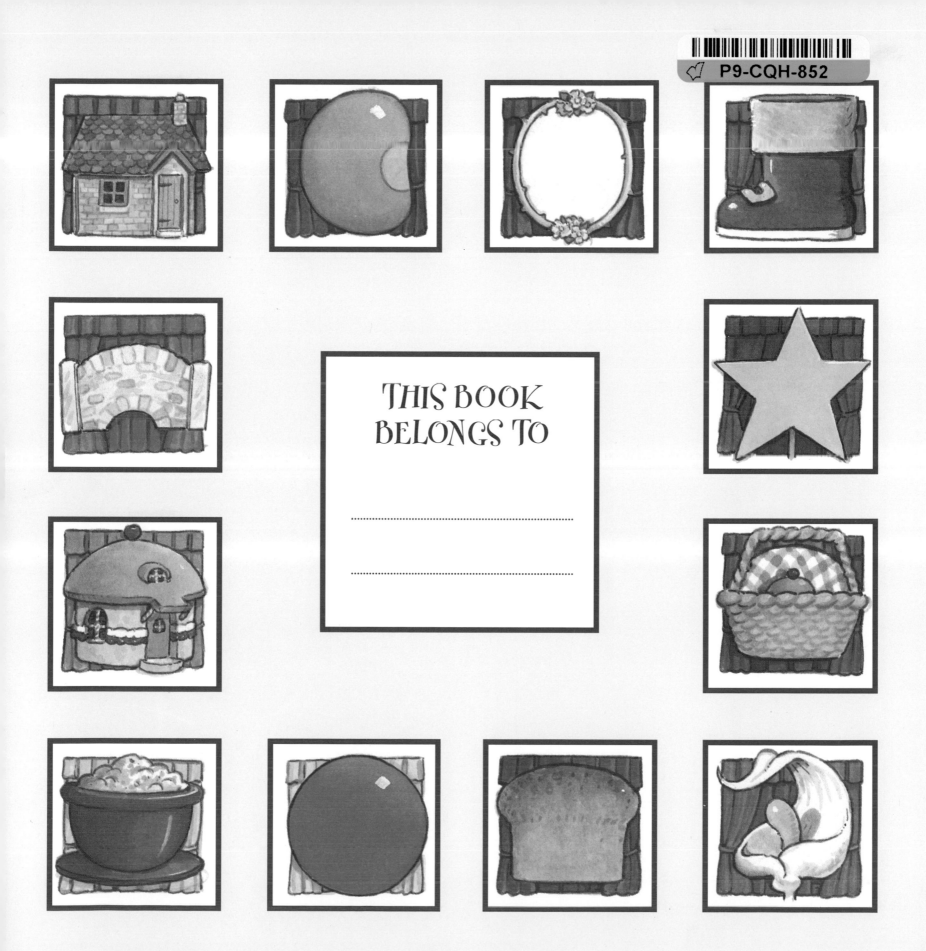

THIS BOOK
BELONGS TO

....

....

MY BIG BOOK OF
FAIRY TALES

MY BIG BOOK OF FAIRY TALES

by Peter Stevenson

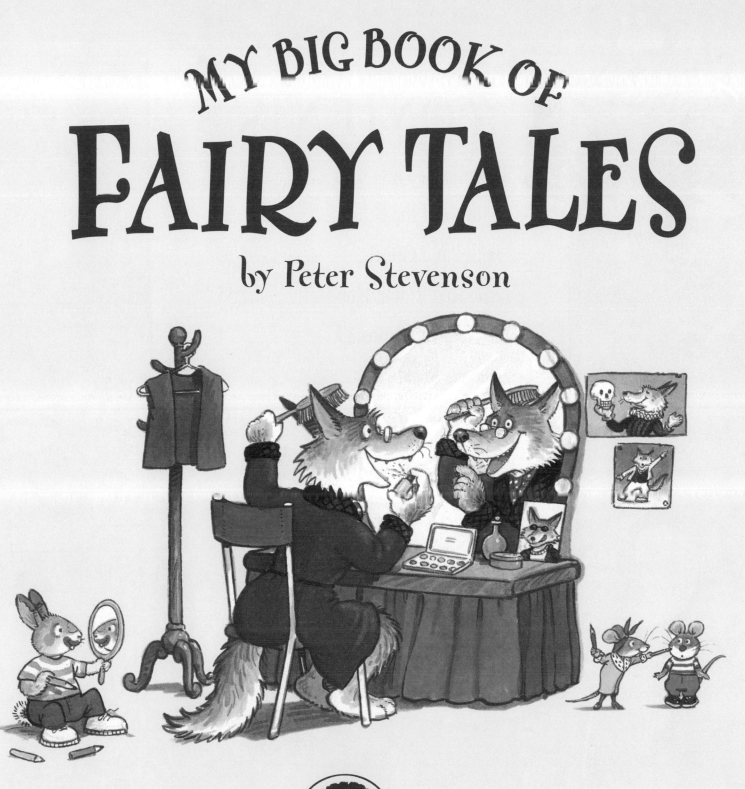

Sandy Creek

CONTENTS

Illustrated by Peter Stevenson
Re-told by Louisa Somerville

© 2001 by Fernleigh Books

This 2009 edition published by Sandy Creek by arrangement with Fernleigh Books,
1A London Road, Enfield, Middlesex, EN2 6BN, England

Sandy Creek Books, 122 Fifth Avenue, New York, NY 10011

ISBN-13: 978-0-7607-3500-8

Printed and bound in Dubai O011 June 2009.

7   9   10   8

Material in this edition was previously published in the Puppet Theater series.

THREE LITTLE PIGS

Once upon a time, there lived a mother pig who had three children. At first, they were a happy family. But every day, the three little pigs grew bigger and noisier. The first little pig beat a drum all day long. The second little pig played a recorder, and the third little pig strummed a guitar. They only stopped to watch rock videos on television!

One day Mother Pig couldn't stand the noise any longer. "This house is too small for all of us," she said. "You must go and find homes of your own. Then you can make as much noise as you like!"

So the three little pigs kissed their mother goodbye and set off into the world.

After the pigs had walked for a long time, the first little pig started to feel rather tired. Just then, a farmer went by with a cartload of straw.

"Excuse me, sir," said the first little pig. "That straw looks light enough and soft enough for me to build myself a house. May I have some?"

"Help yourself," replied the man. So the little pig set to work to build himself a home. He worked hard all day, making himself a fine house of straw, with a fine thatched roof.

Soon he had finished his house and had moved in.

The first little pig settled down in his chair, switched on his favorite music and got ready to play his drum. Just then, he got a terrible shock. A face appeared at the window! It was a big bad wolf, who had been watching him all along.

"He'll make a tasty meal," the wolf mumbled to himself. Then he called out, "Little pig, little pig, let me come in."

"No, no, no!" squealed the first little pig. "Not by the hairs on my chinny chin chin – I WILL NOT let you in!"

"Then," said the big bad wolf, "I'll huff, and I'll puff, and I'll blow your house down!" And sure enough, the wolf gave a little HUFF, and he gave a little PUFF, and he blew the house of straw right down. The little pig and all his belongings were tossed high in the air before landing with a thump on the ground.

"Now I'll have you for dinner, little pig!" cried the wolf.

"No, you won't!" the little pig squealed, and even before the straw had settled, he was off as fast as his little legs would carry him.

"Hee, hee, hee!" the big bad wolf chuckled to himself, and gnashed his teeth with glee. "I think I smell bacon. Mmmm...delicious!"

Meanwhile, the second little pig had come across a woodcutter
chopping wood in the forest.

"Excuse me, sir," said the second pig. "That wood looks
light enough and smooth enough for me to build myself a house.
Will you be so kind as to give me some?"

"Certainly," said the man.

So the second pig set to work to make himself a home.
He worked hard, and soon he had built
a fine wooden house, with a fine wooden roof. He found
that he even had enough wood left over to make
himself a comfortable bed and a chair, too. Just
as he had finished his house, his little brother
came running up, all out of breath.

"Beware the big bad wolf!"
the first little pig cried.

The two little pigs were very frightened. Soon the wolf came along and shouted, "Little pigs, little pigs, let me come in!"

"No, no, no!" cried the trembling pigs. "Not by the hairs on our chinny chin chins – WE WILL NOT let you in!"

13

"We'll see about that!" growled the big bad wolf. "I'll huff, and I'll puff, and I'll blow your house down!" And the wolf gave a little HUFF, and he gave a little PUFF, and he did blow that house down. The two little pigs and their belongings were tossed high in the air before landing on the ground with a crash!

"Quick! Let's get out of here before the wolf has us both for dinner!" squealed the two little pigs. And they ran away as fast as their short legs could carry them.

"Hee, hee, hee!" the mean old wolf laughed to himself. Then he skipped after the pigs, whistling a happy tune.

"Bacon, sausages, and ham, I'm ready for dinner – yes, I am!" sang the wolf.

In the meantime, the third little pig had met a builder with a wheelbarrow full of bricks.

"Please, sir," said the third pig politely. "Those bricks look strong enough and smooth enough for me to build myself a house. Would you be so kind as to let me have some?"

"Of course," said the man.

The third little pig worked hard all day making his home. He built himself a fine strong house of bricks, with a fine fireplace, a fine chimney, and a strong tiled roof. He worked so fast that he had finished his house long before sunset and even had time to bake a batch of cupcakes. Just then, along came his two little brothers.

"Beware the big bad wolf!" they cried.

"I'm not scared of him," replied the third little pig.

15

The third pig calmly invited his frightened little brothers inside.
They sat down to glasses of milk and a big plate of iced
cupcakes. Just as the third little pig took a bite, the hungry
wolf looked through the window.

"Little pigs, little pigs, let me come in!" he yelled.

But the third pig shouted back, "Go away, you silly old wolf!"
His brothers looked at him, amazed.

"Whatever shall we do now?" they gasped.

The wolf's stomach was rumbling and he was very hungry. He was getting very angry, too. He gave a little HUFF, and he gave a little PUFF, but he could NOT blow this house down. Then he gave a bigger HUFF, and he gave a bigger PUFF, but still he could not blow the house down.

"Ha, ha, ha!" the pigs laughed. They watched through the window, as the wolf's cheeks turned redder and redder. Now he was very hungry and very angry indeed!

17

The big bad wolf grew ANGRIER and ANGRIER! He was determined to EAT the little pigs one way or another.

"Fat pork chops with dumpling stew, I'm going to get my paws on you!" chanted the wolf. Then he saw the big wide chimney on top of the little brick house, and he had an idea.

He started to climb up the strong brick wall of the third little pig's house. Then he scrambled up the strong tiled roof and danced along the ridge towards the chimney. The three little pigs looked up at the ceiling as they heard the wolf crashing about on the roof.

"I will get my dinner somehow," he said, chuckling to himself, as he looked down the chimney into the fireplace.

The first two pigs clung to each other, terrified. But the third little pig guessed what the wolf's plan was, and he said to his brothers,

"Quick! Put more wood on the fire." The three pigs rushed about to make the biggest roaring fire they could. They put all the wood that was left over from making the windows and doors of the third little pig's house, but the fire wasn't hot enough.

So the first little pig threw his drum onto the fire. The second little pig threw his recorder onto the fire. Then the third little pig threw his guitar onto the fire. At last the fire was roaring hot.

"It's dinnertime! Come and get us!" they called up the chimney gleefully to the big bad wolf.

The wolf heard the three little pigs calling.

"You're right. It's dinnertime!" he shouted. Without a second thought, he slid all the way down the chimney and fell into the fire.

"HELP, HELP!" he cried. "My tail is on FIRE!" He raced out of the pig's house and down the road, and that was the last that the three little pigs ever saw of the big bad wolf.

"Yippee!" they cried and hugged each other for joy.

The three little pigs knew that the big bad wolf would never bother them again, so they decided to build themselves a big new house to live in together. They built the walls of strong brick. They thatched the roof with soft straw. Then they made comfortable furniture out of smooth wood. They were so happy that they decided to throw a big party.

They went out shopping to replace the instruments that they had thrown into the fire. The first little pig bought a drum kit. The second little pig bought a saxophone and the third little pig bought an electric guitar.

Then they went home and had a very noisy party with their friends – but no one else could hear them, because their house of brick and wood and straw was so well built.

And what became of the
big bad wolf? Well, he didn't stop
running away from the three little pigs'
house until he came to a river far away.
Then he plunged his burning tail
into the icy water to cool it.
He came out shivering and bedraggled
and feeling very sorry for himself.
"I'm still feeling hungry," said the wolf.
"But I'm definitely not in the mood
for a bacon sandwich!"

BEAUTY
AND THE
BEAST

A poor merchant went to collect some cargo from a ship. His daughter, Beauty, asked him to bring her back a rose. But the ship left port early, so he started for home empty-handed. As night fell, he came upon a dark castle.

The merchant knocked at the door, but nobody answered.

The door was unlocked, so he went inside. There he found a room prepared for a guest. "How strange," he said to himself. "These must be friendly people. I'm sure I can stay one night."

So he settled down to sleep.

The next morning, the merchant found breakfast laid out for him in the dining room. After eating his fill, he left the castle, and found himself in a beautiful rose garden.

"At least I can take Beauty the present I promised her," the merchant thought, as he broke off a single stem. At that very moment, he heard a fearful howl. Coming towards him was a hideous beast. The man screamed in terror.

"How dare you steal a rose?" growled the beast. "To pay for this, you must send me the first person you see on arriving home to be my companion." The merchant was too terrified to refuse.

"I w-will," he stammered.

The merchant arrived home and was met by his daughter. She welcomed him and gave him tea and cakes to eat by the fire she had lit. He gave her the rose he had picked, but her delight turned to sorrow as, reluctantly, he explained what had happened. He told her about his night in the castle, about picking the rose, and about his encounter with the beast.

"I have to send you to live with this horrible beast," he said, miserably, "but I can't bear to think of what I have agreed to. If only I could go in your place," he wept.

"Do not be sad, Father," Beauty said. "I will go. I am sure that there must be some good in this poor beast."

27

The day arrived for Beauty to go to the beast's castle. Sadly, she said goodbye to her father, who was weeping bitterly.

"You are more precious than my own life. Let me go instead," he begged.

"No, Father, it is I who must go," Beauty replied, "and I am sure all will be well."

She set off through the forest all alone, and at last she arrived at the beast's castle. She knocked at the door, but no one came to answer, so she let herself in, just as her father had done.

Then she searched all around the castle, but to her surprise, never saw another soul.

Beauty did her best to be happy. The castle was well looked after, and there was always good food to eat and a soft bed to sleep in. But try as she might, she couldn't help feeling lonely.

"I just wish there was someone to keep me company," Beauty sighed. She thought that she was being watched, but she never saw the beast. Sometimes she would see a shadow fall in the light from a doorway. At other times, she thought she saw a figure reflected in a mirror.

Days passed and still she had not caught sight of the beast. Beauty began to wonder whether he really existed, or if she was dreaming all of this.

One day, as Beauty sat in the rose garden, a dark shadow
fell upon her. She heard a terrible growling, and then a voice said,
   "Come and walk with me." Beauty looked up to see the beast for
the first time. He was even uglier than she had expected
and she felt very frightened. However, she answered
as bravely as she could, "Of course I will."
   The beast extended a hairy paw towards her. She was surprised
to find that he took her gently by the hand and led her through the
garden. They strolled around and
admired the flowers. To
her astonishment,
Beauty found that the
beast seemed to know a lot
about gardening.

As the days passed, Beauty learned that the beast was not as fearsome as he had seemed, and they often walked and talked together. Slowly, they became friends.

Beauty realized that for all his ugliness, the beast was a kind and gentle soul who took good care of her, and she became fond of him. "I'm grateful for the kindness that you have shown me," she said.

However, Beauty was still sad. One evening, they were eating dinner together. As usual, the beast had laid out a fine feast with all kinds of good things to eat and drink.

Beauty sat at the table, but she had no appetite. Soon she pushed her plate away.

"What's wrong?" the beast asked. Beauty plucked up all her courage and said to him, "I miss my father. If only I could see him and know that he's well. I fear that perhaps he is not." The beast pulled out a mirror and gave it to her.

"Look into this mirror and you will see whatever you wish," said the beast. Beauty looked into the mirror and saw her father lying ill in bed.

"I must go to him," she gasped. "He is all alone and he needs me." With great sadness, the beast allowed her to return to her home. As she left the castle, he pressed the mirror into her hand.

"Take my mirror and look into it and think of me sometimes," he pleaded.

"I can't live without you," he added.

So Beauty returned home, where she found her father gravely ill. She was shocked to see the state he was in.

"Oh, Father," she cried, falling to her knees beside his bed. "If only I'd known you were ill, I'd have come home sooner."

"Just to see you is cure enough," her father said smiling. At the sight of his daughter, he started to feel better. Soon he was out of bed and fully recovered. Beauty reassured her father that the beast had treated her kindly and with respect. However, the mirror lay abandoned, and Beauty was so busy nursing her father that she forgot to look into it to see the beast, as he had asked.

The days went by and Beauty and her father were very happy together. Then one day Beauty came across the mirror. Suddenly she remembered her promise to the beast. She looked into the mirror and, to her horror, saw the beast lying very still in his rose garden.

"I must return to the beast, Father," she cried. "I fear that he is dying." Tearfully, she embraced her father. Then she raced through the forest to be with the beast.

"Oh dear," she thought, "I hope that I am not too late to help my poor Beast." When Beauty reached the rose garden, she saw that the beast was lying there, just as she had seen in the mirror.

Beauty rushed over to the beast and fell to her knees beside him. He lay so still that she feared the very worst. For now she remembered that he had said that he could not live without her.

"Please don't die, my darling Beast," she wept. "I know that I abandoned you. But now I have returned to be at your side. I love you with all my heart." And then she leaned over to kiss him.

Suddenly, before her very eyes, the beast began to shake violently. He swayed from side to side and his head began to spin. "W-what's happening?" she stuttered. For now Beauty could see that he was changing shape...

...into the most handsome prince.

"Oh!" cried Beauty.

"Oh, Beauty," cried the prince. "A cruel fairy turned me into a beast until a time when a good and beautiful woman would fall in love with me. You have broken the spell I was under, and now I can be myself again. Will you marry me?"

"Yes, I will," replied Beauty, as the prince put his arms around her and kissed her.

Beauty's father was overjoyed to hear the news, and the happy couple were married the very next day. The three of them lived happily ever after in the prince's castle.

And although she knew that it wasn't really his name, Beauty couldn't help fondly calling the prince "Beast" for the rest of their lives!

HANSEL
AND GRETEL

Long ago, there were two children – a boy named Hansel and a girl named Gretel. They lived with their father, who was a woodcutter, in a little cottage on the edge of a deep wood. They were very poor.

Although their mother had died, their father loved them and took good care of them. Hansel and Gretel were happy to spend all day long playing outside the cottage. Then one day, their father married again.

"Come children, meet your new stepmother," the woodcutter said. Hansel and Gretel didn't like the look of her one little bit. Their father was so much in love with his new wife that he was unaware she was really a witch.

"*Hmm!*" muttered the woman. "We have very little food to eat. I will put a spell on my husband to make him take the children into the woods and leave them there. Then at least we won't starve!"

Soon the children and their father set off into the woods.

Sure enough, their father left
them behind! But Hansel guessed
what his stepmother had planned,
and dropped white pebbles
along their path.
"We'll follow the trail of
pebbles all the way
home," he said
to Gretel.

The next day the children were led into the woods again. This time, Hansel grabbed a loaf of bread as he left the house. In the woods, he secretly left a trail of bread crumbs behind. Soon he and Gretel were lost once again!

"Don't worry," said Hansel. "The bread trail will get us home." But there was not a crumb in sight.

"Oh, no!" cried Gretel. "The birds have eaten them all. Now we'll never find our way home."

"Don't give up so soon,"
said Hansel to his sister.
They walked and walked
until at last they came to
a clearing in the forest.
"Oh, look!" Gretel shouted
excitedly.
"A house made of candy!"
cried Hansel.

The children were so hungry that they rushed up to the candy cottage and started to break off pieces to eat.

"Delicious!" shouted Gretel, cramming her mouth with cake.

"Scrumptious!" agreed Hansel, as he ate a candy cane.

The children were so busy eating that they didn't notice a witch who was watching them. Suddenly, the witch jumped out of the cottage and grabbed them.

"How dare you eat my house!" she cackled.

Before the children could explain, the witch
pushed Hansel into a cage in the garden.
Then she made Gretel cook meals and
clean the house. She kept Hansel in
the cage and gave him good things to eat.
"When you are fatter I am going to
eat you!" she said with a grin, and
poked him with her pointed fork.
Gretel watched her
brother helplessly.
How could she
set him free?

But Hansel had his own plan. Every day the witch checked to see if he was fat enough to eat.

"Hansel, put out your finger," the witch would say. Luckily for Hansel, she could not see very well. In fact, she couldn't see further than her nose. Whenever she leaned into the cage, Hansel would hold out an old chicken bone for her to feel.

"No, still too bony," the witch would mutter to herself, thinking it was his finger.

"WHEW!" said Hansel when the witch had gone. "She still doesn't suspect a thing."

The witch couldn't understand why Hansel didn't seem to be getting any fatter. Eventually she got tired of waiting.

"Ready or not, I'm going to eat you tomorrow, little boy," she cackled. The next day she said to Gretel,

"Light the oven, little girl, so that I can cook your brother for supper!"

"Yes, ma'am," was all that Gretel could stutter. Now it was Gretel's turn to think of a plan.

Gretel did as she was told as slowly as possible. She could not bear the thought of what was about to happen to her brother. But soon the witch became impatient.

"Climb in and see if the oven is hot enough!" she told Gretel. But Gretel was smart. She went up to the oven and pretended to get her head stuck in the door.

"I can't seem to get in," she said. "My head is much too big. Can you show me how, please?"

"What nonsense!" screamed the witch. "A little girl's head will fit inside the oven perfectly well. Look, even I can fit my head inside!" She pushed Gretel aside and leaned over to look inside the oven.

With all her might, Gretel quickly pushed the witch into the oven and slammed the door shut with a great BANG! Then she fastened the bolt.

"Got you, you horrid old witch!" yelled Gretel.

How the witch howled! Gretel didn't wait to listen. She ran out into the garden.

It didn't take Gretel long to find the key to the iron cage.
She opened the door and let her brother out.

"We're free at last!" shouted the children,
hugging each other and dancing round the garden.
Together they explored the witch's house. In her
bedroom, they found a trunk full of gold, silver,
necklaces, and jewels, and there was more
jewelery hidden under
the witch's quilt.

"We're rich! We're rich!"
they laughed.
"Wait until Father
sees all this!"
cried Gretel.

Just then, there was a noise at the door. The children rushed downstairs and were overjoyed to see their father there.

"Hansel, Gretel!" he cried, clasping the children to him.

"Father," they cried, "look what we found. We're rich!"

"Oh, my…!" he exclaimed, amazed at the treasure.

"But how did you find us?" asked Hansel.

Their father explained that the witch was really their wicked stepmother, who had deserted him. The moment that Gretel had pushed her into the oven, the spell on him had been broken, and he had gone looking for his children in the forest.

Hansel, Gretel, and their father filled their pockets full of treasure. Then they returned to their little tumbledown cottage at the edge of the forest. They had enough money now for their father to repair the cottage and make it warm and cozy, and to buy himself a shiny new car. "Now let's have a party!" he cried. So he drove into town and bought all sorts of good things to eat. And they had a wonderful party.

"We'll never be poor
or hungry again," said Father.
"No, never," the children replied.
And they all lived happily ever after.
And as for the wicked witch?
She was not dead after all, but she
flew away on her broomstick
and was never seen again.

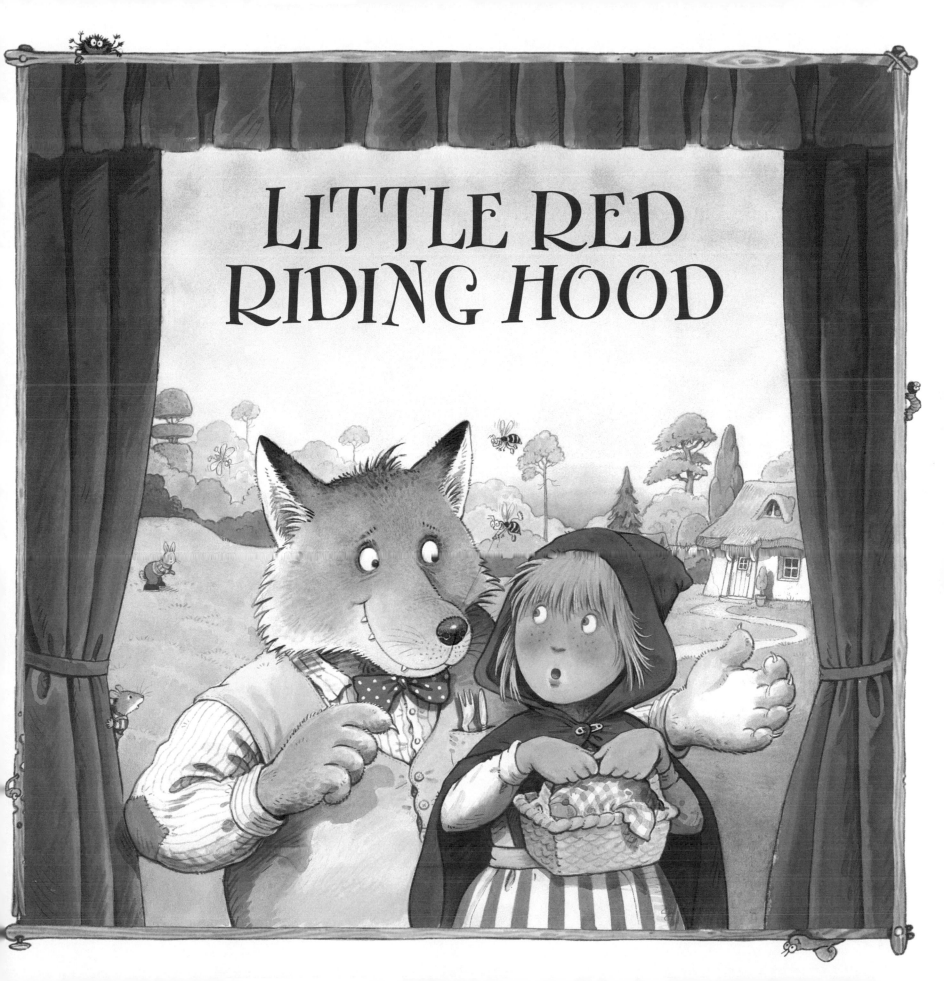

LITTLE RED
RIDING HOOD

nce there lived a young girl who was known as
Little Red Riding Hood because of the red cape
that her grandmother had made for her. One lovely
summer morning, Little Red Riding Hood waved goodbye to her
mother and set off into the woods. She was on her way to take
some freshly baked cakes to her grandmother, who was sick.

"See you later, Mom," she called out.

As Little Red Riding Hood
skipped through the woods, a
sly wolf greeted her with a smile.
"And where are you off to,
little girl?" said the wolf.
"To my grandmother's house,"
she replied and skipped on.

The wolf was clever. He
called out to Little Red Riding
Hood in his sweetest voice,
"Why not stop and pick
a lovely bunch of flowers to take to
your grandma as well?"

"What a good idea!" said Little Red
Riding Hood, bending down to pick
the sweet blooms. Right away, the
wicked wolf decided to take
a shortcut to Grandma's cottage.

"First I'll get rid of Granny –
and then I'll have Little Red
Riding Hood for lunch," he declared.
And off he raced by another path.

Soon the wolf was knocking at Grandma's cottage door.

"It's me, Little Red Riding Hood, Grandma," said the wolf in a high-pitched little voice, "and I've brought you a basket of cakes and some flowers."

"Come in, my dear," said Grandma. The wolf crept into Grandma's bedroom, where she lay tucked up in bed.

"How tasty you look," said the wolf.

"AIYEE!" Grandma screamed, and dashed into a cupboard. The wolf put on Grandma's nightcap and nightgown. Then he climbed into her bed to wait for Little Red Riding Hood.

Soon Little Red Riding Hood came along, skipping down the path to the cottage.

"It's so quiet," she murmured to herself, looking all around. The birds were not singing quite as prettily as when she had set off from home. The sun was not shining as brightly. She felt a chill in the air.

She knocked at the door.
"Grandma, I've
brought you some
cakes," she called out.
"Come in, my dear,"
growled a deep voice.
"Grandma's voice is
strange," she thought.

61

The door swung open with a slow CREAK and Little Red Riding Hood stepped inside. "Hello, Grandma," she said. "How are you feeling? You sound awful."

Grandma was tucked deep under the covers of her bed
with her nightcap pulled down low over her face.
Little Red Riding Hood stood a little way from the bed.
   "Oh, Grandma," she cried, forgetting her manners,
"what a BIG nose you have!" The wolf smiled.
   "Well, that's all the better for smelling your lovely
cakes with, my dear.
Come closer so that
I can see you better,"
croaked the wolf.

Little Red Riding Hood came a little closer to the bed.
The wicked wolf's eyes glittered in the lamplight.
She thought they looked different from her grandmother's eyes.

"Oh, Grandma," she cried, "what very BIG and
watery eyes you have." Then she saw the wolf's big, bushy
eyebrows peeping out from under the nightcap.

"And your eyebrows are so BUSHY!" she added.

"Don't worry about my big eyes," said the wolf.
"That makes them all the better to see you with, my
dear child." Little Red Riding Hood still felt nervous,
however. There was still something
about Grandma that
wasn't right. But what
could it be?

Little Red Riding Hood came closer still and the wolf grinned a wide smile at her. She noticed a row of very large, white, pointed teeth. She thought they looked different from Grandma's teeth. She came up close so that she was next to the wolf's head on the pillow.

"Grandma," she squealed in terror, "your teeth are so HUGE and POINTY!"

The wolf pulled down the blankets, grinned a great big grin, and bared all his huge, white, pointed teeth.

"All the better to EAT YOU WITH!" the wolf yelled. And he began to growl a terrible growl. He sniffed the air with his great long nose and stared at Little Red Riding Hood with his big eyes. Then he licked his chops with his great big tongue.

"I'm coming to get you!" he screamed at Little Red Riding Hood, as she backed away.

And with that, the wolf leaped out of Grandma's bed.

"What a lovely snack you will make, my dear," he growled as he flew through the air towards Little Red Riding Hood. Little Red Riding Hood dropped her basket of cakes to the floor.

"HELP! HELP!" she screamed at the top of her voice, but there was no one to save her.

Just as the wolf was about to gobble her up, a kind woodsman burst through the door. He had heard Little Red Riding Hood's cries for help. He lifted his axe.

"Come here, you sly old wolf!" he yelled.

"Time for me to GO!" said the wolf.

The woodsman chased the wolf off into the woods. Then Grandma burst out of the cupboard. She and Little Red Riding Hood hugged each other and cried for joy.

"Let's hope that mean old wolf has learned his lesson this time," said Little Red Riding Hood, as she watched him run down the path with the woodsman close behind.

"I don't think that big bad wolf will ever bother us again!" replied Grandma.

As he ran through the forest, the wolf struggled to get out of Grandma's nightgown and nightcap. Eventually, he tore himself free of her clothes and disappeared into the darkness of the woods.

Later that day, the woodsman brought Grandma's nightgown and nightcap back to her. As for the wolf, well, he was never seen again. And Little Red Riding Hood and Grandma lived happily ever after.

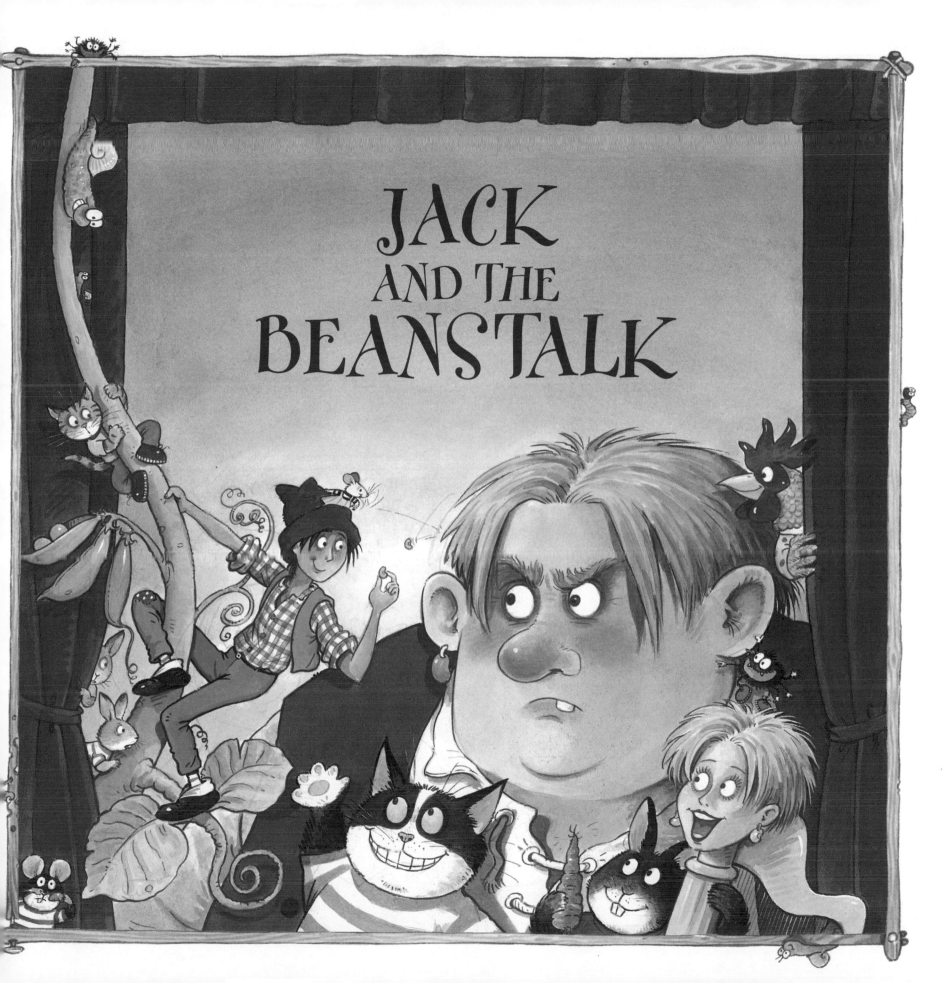

JACK
AND THE
BEANSTALK

Once upon a time there was an old woman who lived in a tumbledown cottage with her only son, Jack. They grew poorer and poorer until one day all they had left was their cow.

"Jack," said his mother. "You must take the cow to market and sell her – or we shall starve. And mind you get a good price for her!"

The next morning, Jack set off for the market on his bicycle with the cow trotting along behind on a rope.

Along the road Jack met a man passing by. The man looked at the cow, then he said to the lad,

"Will you swap your cow for some beans?"

"No," Jack replied, "I must sell my cow at the market so that I can buy food to eat."

"But these are magic beans," said the man, reaching into his pocket and pulling out a few old brown beans.

"Scatter them on the ground and they'll make your fortune!"

So in the end, Jack agreed to swap his cow for a handful of old brown beans.

Jack put the beans
in his pocket and
went home.

"Look what I've got!"
he shouted to his mother,
holding out his handful of beans.

But the old woman screeched,
"Is that all you got for my precious cow?"
She was so angry that she snatched
the beans and threw them out of the
window. She scolded her son and sent
him to bed without so much
as a crust of bread.

Next morning, Jack woke to find a gigantic beanstalk had grown outside his bedroom window during the night. He ran out of the cottage to get a better look. The beanstalk was so huge that the top of it disappeared into the clouds.

"I'm going to climb up to the top and seek my fortune," Jack said to himself. And he started climbing up the beanstalk. "Come back, Jack!" called his mother. But higher and higher up went Jack.

At last Jack reached the top of the beanstalk. He looked up to see an enormous castle. Outside the castle door sat a huge giantess. Jack was so hungry that he walked straight up to her and said, "Please, will you give me something to eat? I'm starving."

"All right," replied the giantess, who was feeling sorry for the lad. "But you'd better watch out. If my husband catches sight of you, he'll gobble you up!"

The giantess beckoned Jack inside the castle and gave him a huge bowl of soup. Just as Jack was eating the last tasty drop, he felt the castle shudder with the approach of thunderous footsteps.

"Quick! Hide!" whispered the giantess. Jack slipped behind a mug of tea. In came the giant, sniffing the air.

"Fee-fi-fo-fum, I smell the blood of an Englishman! Be he alive or be he dead, I'll grind his bones to make my bread!" roared the giant.

77

"Nonsense!" said his wife. "It's your dinner you can smell."
Satisfied with the answer, the giant sat down and began
to count out his gold into two bags. It seemed to take
forever, as he counted very slowly. At last he yawned and
sat back in his chair. Soon he was fast asleep and snoring.
Quick as a flash, Jack sneaked across the table.

He grabbed one of the bags
of gold. It was so heavy
that he had to drag it to
the edge of the table
and then onto the floor.
He dragged the gold out
of the castle and all the
way back to the beanstalk.

Jack scrambled down the beanstalk with the heavy bag of gold on his back.

"Mother, we're rich!" he cried, as he reached the cottage door and poured the gold coins out at her feet. The old woman hugged her son for joy.

"We have enough gold to last us for the rest of our lives. We're wealthy now beyond our wildest dreams. So don't ever climb that beanstalk again, Jack!" she warned her son.

Jack nodded. But he knew that he wanted more treasure.

The very next morning Jack climbed up the beanstalk again. Once again, there was the giantess sitting outside the castle door.

"Please shelter me," he begged her. The giantess couldn't help but feel sorry for the lad once more, so she beckoned him inside. Soon he felt the castle shudder and heard the giant shouting at the top of his voice,

"Fee-fi-fo-fum, I smell the blood of an Englishman! Be he alive or be he dead, I'll grind his bones to make my bread!"

The giant's wife brought him
a speckled hen. "Lay!" ordered the
giant. The hen laid a beautiful
golden egg. The giant put
the egg in his pocket
and fell asleep.

Jack tiptoed across to the table. Then he picked up the hen and made off with her down the beanstalk. Jack's mother was overjoyed to see the great pile of golden eggs that the hen laid outside her door.

"We have all we need now, what with the bag of gold and the golden eggs. Don't climb that beanstalk again! And don't disobey me this time!" his mother scolded.

The very next morning, however, Jack couldn't resist climbing up the beanstalk just once more. The last time, he promised himself.

Jack waited until the giantess came out with a bucket, then he tiptoed into the castle. Soon the castle walls began to shake and Jack heard the giant roar,

"Fee-fi-fo-fum, I smell the blood of an Englishman! Be he alive or be he dead, I'll grind his bones to make my bread!" The giant sat down and called for his wife to bring him his golden harp.

"Sing!" ordered the giant. The harp began to sing the most beautiful song. At first, the giant listened to the harp's lovely music, but soon he fell asleep as usual.

Jack sprang across the room and seized the harp.
But as he made off with it, the harp began to wail,
"Master! Master! Help! I'm being stolen!"
The giant awoke and, with a mighty roar, chased
after Jack as he headed for the beanstalk with
the harp under his arm. As he climbed down
the beanstalk, Jack could hear the
giant close behind him. The further
down he climbed, the closer the
giant was behind him.
As he reached the bottom,
Jack shouted out,
    "Mother! Quick!
Fetch the axe!"

Jack's mother ran to fetch the axe. As soon as Jack reached the ground, she began to chop furiously at the beanstalk. Chop, chop, chop went the axe until finally there was a great sound of ripping, and the beanstalk tore in half.

The giant was left hanging on to the top half of the stalk. There was nothing he could do except shake his fist and shout angrily in his rage.

But what with the two bags of gold, a hen that laid golden eggs, and a golden harp that sang, Jack's mother was more than contented and readily forgave her son's disobedience.

Jack and his mother
were now rich beyond
their wildest dreams.
"Let's buy a car, mother!" said Jack.
So first they bought a car and then they
found they had enough money left over
to buy back their beloved old cow –
and plenty more besides. And Jack,
his mother, the cow, and
the speckled hen lived
happily ever after.

SLEEPING
BEAUTY

Once upon a time, a queen was christening her baby daughter. She had invited twelve fairies to be godmothers. The queen held a fabulous feast in celebration, and the fairies were having a wonderful time.

Soon it was time for each godmother to give the baby princess a gift. One by one, the fairies stepped up to the cradle to greet the child. The first fairy gave her the gift of beauty, the second presented her with generosity. Others gave her happiness and health.

Just when the queen thought her daughter had everything she needed, the doors were thrown open and a powerful and nasty fairy flew in. The queen gasped in shock – she had forgotten to invite her.

"How dare you forget me?" raged the fairy. "I, too, have a gift for your daughter! When she is sixteen years old, she will prick her finger on a spindle and die."

The fairy stormed out, leaving the queen in floods of tears.

"Wait," said a tiny voice. "All is not lost. I haven't given my gift yet." The queen looked up to see the smallest fairy of all standing by the crib.

"I can't undo that spell," the fairy said, "but I can change it a little. My present to your daughter is the gift of love. She will not die, but she will sleep for a hundred years until love comes to rescue her. She will be woken by the kiss of a prince who truly loves her."

Well, the smallest fairy's gift was certainly better than nothing, so the queen dried her tears. However, she still could not believe that the smallest fairy's wish might come true. She set about ordering that all the spindles in the kingdom be destroyed.

The little princess gurgled happily in her cradle, unaware of the drama going on. But the queen slept not a wink that night, for fear of what might happen to her child.

Sixteen years passed, and
the princess had grown
up beautiful and happy,
healthy and generous.
She was also quite
inquisitive, and one day
she was wandering about
the castle when she came
to a door she'd never
noticed before.
She opened it
and went into
the room.

There was an old woman sitting at a spindle, spinning beautiful thread. Now the princess had never seen a spindle before, as all those in the land had been destroyed. Curiosity drove her towards the old woman.

"Ooh, that looks fun. Let me have a go," said the princess. But as she stepped forward, she tripped over the old woman's cat. She fell towards the spindle needle and pricked her middle finger. A deep red drop of blood fell on the floor.

Immediately, the princess sank down to the floor and fell into a deep sleep.

In that very same instant, everyone in the castle fell asleep, too. The cooks fell asleep as they tended the roasting spit in the kitchen, and the horses fell asleep in the stable yard with their riders still in their saddles. The queen, who had been taking tea and cakes at the card table, leaned back heavily in her chair, fell soundly asleep, and started to snore.

The cat fell asleep as it was about to pounce on a mouse. And even the mouse slept soundly.

Only the two fairies were still awake – and they were arguing about who was the most powerful.

Then something even stranger happened. The ground seemed to heave, and suddenly a thousand thorny roses burst through and climbed the castle walls, covering it in a beautiful, scented barrier. Soon nothing of the castle could be seen, except for the very tallest turret.

The years passed and the thorns around the castle grew thicker and thicker. At the same time, the legend of the bad fairy's curse upon the Sleeping Beauty spread to lands far and wide.

As time went by, many brave princes tried to cut down the briars, but not one succeeded. Countless young men lost their lives in the forest of thorns.

One day, a hundred years after the princess had pricked her finger, a handsome prince came riding towards the castle. He had seen Sleeping Beauty in a dream and his heart went out to her in true love. He was determined to be the one to cut his way through the thorns, but as he looked at the castle from a distance, he could not imagine how he would possibly achieve this.

The prince looked at the beautiful and strange tangle
of roses and thorns.

"I wonder why they are there?" he asked himself.
But as he crossed the bridge towards them,
a strange and wonderful thing happened.
The roses parted in front of him until
he could see the castle doors.

The prince made his way cautiously inside the castle. The sight that met his eyes made him gasp. There were bodies all over the place. Some were slumped over tables. Others lay on chairs. At first he thought everyone was dead, until he heard the guards snoring.

"They're all sleeping!" the prince whispered to himself. He tiptoed around, fearing that they might wake, and made his way up the stairs. At last he came to the room where the princess lay.

"Oh, she is so lovely," whispered the prince, as he gazed down at Sleeping Beauty. He couldn't resist leaning over and giving her a tiny kiss. Straight away, the princess opened her eyes and smiled.

"You took your time," she said. "But what a great way to wake up. How long have I been asleep, by the way?" she added, yawning and rubbing her eyes.

"A hundred years – but don't worry. You haven't aged a bit," replied the prince. "It's time to get up now," he continued, taking her gently by the hand.

The prince picked the princess up and carried her downstairs. All around were the sounds of people waking up: the cooks were clattering around the kitchen, the horses were whinnying in the stables, and the queen shouted, "I win!" None of them realized they had been asleep for a hundred years.

"Hello, Mama," said the princess. "Sorry I overslept."

"Overslept?" replied the queen, looking puzzled.
"But I'd only just settled down to cards ... anyway, who's
your friend?" she continued, eyeing the prince suspiciously.

"Oh, this is my handsome prince and I'm going to
marry him, if that's all right with you," said the princess.

"That will be just perfect," said the queen,
"as long as you don't
invite any bad fairies
to the wedding!"

So the prince and Sleeping Beauty
were married the next day. They invited
the queen and everyone
else at the castle and all the good
fairies to the wedding, and they
lived happily ever after.
And I'm glad to say that the
nasty fairy did not turn up at
the wedding. In fact, she
was never seen again.

BILLY GOATS GRUFF

A long time ago, there were three billy goats who lived together in a rocky field on one side of a valley.

There was a baby billy goat called Little Billy Goat Gruff, his big sister called Middle Billy Goat Gruff, and their big brother, whose name was Big Billy Goat Gruff.

The three Billy Goats Gruff had eaten all the grass on the hill where they lived and they were still hungry.

"I'm starving!" said Big Billy Goat Gruff in his big deep voice.

"Me too!" said Middle Billy Goat Gruff in a middling voice.

"And me!" squeaked Little Billy Goat Gruff in a very high voice.

Now, on the opposite side of their valley, the grass grew thick and green and juicy. In between the two valleys was a river with a rickety old bridge over it. How the three Billy Goats Gruff longed to trit trot trit across the rickety old bridge to feast on the lovely, long grass on the other side.

"The grass on the other side looks so-o-o delicious!" said Big Billy Goat Gruff, licking his great big jaws.

"I agree!" said Middle Billy Goat Gruff, licking her middling jaws.

"Yummy!" was all Little Billy Goat Gruff could manage to say, as he licked his tiny little jaws and felt his tiny little tummy rumbling.

BUT ... it was not so simple to get to the sweet grass on the other side. The river was too deep and too dangerous for the three Billy Goats Gruff to swim across. Neither could they cross the rickety old bridge because beneath that bridge lived a big, ugly, and very fierce troll who loved to eat billy goats best of all.

"How I'd love to have a billy goat for dinner!" the troll cried, rubbing his big, ugly tummy.

One day the Billy Goats Gruff were so hungry that they could stand it no longer.

"We must make a plan to fool that troll," said Big Billy Goat Gruff. The three goats went away to different parts of the field to think until they each came up with a plan.

Then they put their heads together – but not too close in case their horns locked – and discussed each plan in turn. Big Billy Goat Gruff told his plan first, but the other two slowly shook their heads. Then Middle Billy Goat Gruff told her plan, but the other two slowly shook their heads.

Finally, Little Billy Goat Gruff told his plan and the other two nodded in agreement. It was a very good plan indeed.

The next morning, the big, ugly troll was lurking under the rickety old bridge as usual. He was keeping a sharp watch in case a nice, juicy billy goat should venture onto the bridge. As time went by, the troll began to feel rather sleepy. It was nearly lunchtime and the troll had dozed off under the bridge, when all of a sudden he heard the trit trot trit of tiny hooves on his bridge.

"Who dares to cross MY bridge with their trit trot hooves?" growled the big, ugly troll in the deepest, fiercest voice he could manage.

It was Little Billy Goat Gruff and he began to pretend to tremble with fright.

"Excuse me, sir," he said. "It is only I, Little Billy Goat Gruff. Please don't eat me. I am hardly a mouthful for you, and I'm all skin and bone. My sister, who will be coming along soon, is bigger and plumper and much tastier. She will be much better for you to eat."

The big, ugly troll scratched his big, ugly head and thought hard about what the Little Billy Goat Gruff had said.

Fortunately, the troll was not very intelligent, and so he agreed with Little Billy Goat Gruff.

"Very well," he mumbled, "go ahead and I will wait for your sister. She will make a much finer dinner for me." And so Little Billy Goat Gruff went trit trot trit across the rickety old bridge and off into the field of juicy grass, where he was soon munching away happily.

The troll settled down again underneath the rickety old bridge. It was nearly dinnertime and the troll was getting rather hungry, but finally he dozed off.

All of a sudden, he was woken again by the trit trot trit of a set of bigger hooves than before tramping across the bridge. He leapt up onto the top of the bridge, ready to gobble up whomever might try to get past him.

"Who dares to cross my bridge? I will eat them up – every last little bit," he cried in an even deeper, fiercer voice than last time.

Standing right in the middle of the bridge, as bold as anything, was the Middle Billy Goat Gruff. She pretended to think that the troll was joking.

"Oh don't be silly," she giggled. "I am far too slim to make a meal for you. But my brother Big Billy Goat Gruff is coming soon, and he is just the right size to make a perfect meal for a big, handsome troll like you."

The big, ugly troll scratched his big, ugly head and thought hard about what the Middle Billy Goat Gruff had said. In the end he decided that it made good sense.

"Oh, all right then," moaned the troll, as he rubbed his empty tummy. "I suppose I can last a little longer before I simply starve to death. I will wait for your brother, who will make a much finer dinner for me."

So the Middle Billy Goat Gruff went trit trot trit across the rickety old bridge to join Little Billy Goat Gruff in the lovely green field on the far side of the valley.

The troll settled down again underneath the rickety old bridge. It was nearly sunset and he was getting very hungry indeed, but finally he dozed off.

All of a sudden, the troll was disturbed by the deafening trit trot trit of heavy hooves clattering over his bridge.

"Now I have you," called the greedy troll in the deepest and fiercest voice he had ever used. Then he jumped out to find the Big Billy Goat Gruff standing large as life in the middle of the rickety old bridge.

"What a fine dinner you will make for me!" cried the troll.

But the Big Billy Goat Gruff was not in the least bit scared.

"I am not ready to be a dinner for you, or for anyone else," he bellowed in his deep, gruff voice. And then the troll saw just how very big the Big Billy Goat Gruff was and how sharp his horns looked.

Now it was the troll's turn to be truly scared. In fact, he was terrified. His teeth chattered and his hair stood on end as the Big Billy Goat Gruff stared at him with his yellow eyes and slowly licked his jaws.

"P-p-please go across the bridge, won't you?" stammered the troll.

But the Big Billy Goat Gruff didn't seem to hear the troll. He continued to stare straight at him. Then he put his head down and charged at the troll. Faster and faster he thundered across the rickety old bridge towards the troll. He hit the troll with a huge THUMP and knocked him right off the bridge.

Down, down, down went the troll and landed with a gigantic SPLASH in the fast-flowing river. Then the Big Billy Goat Gruff sauntered across the bridge, whistling as he went. Soon he was munching the sweet grass on the other side of the valley alongside his younger brother and sister.

Now the three Billy Goats Gruff go trit trot tritting over the rickety old bridge every day to the grassy field on the other side of the valley. Funnily enough, with all that sweet grass inside their tummies, they have each become so fat that any of them would make a fine meal for a troll, if only a troll was clever enough to catch them!

"Life is sweet," said Big Billy Goat Gruff in his big voice.

"I agree!" said Middle Billy Goat Gruff in her medium voice.

"Mmmm!" was all Little Billy Goat Gruff could say in his very high voice because his mouth was stuffed full of sweet grass.

And as for the troll?
He was a very sorry sight indeed,
as he pulled himself out of the
river all covered in creepy crawlies.
He hasn't been seen since,
but people say that he declared that
he would never lurk beside
a river in search of his dinner,
ever again.

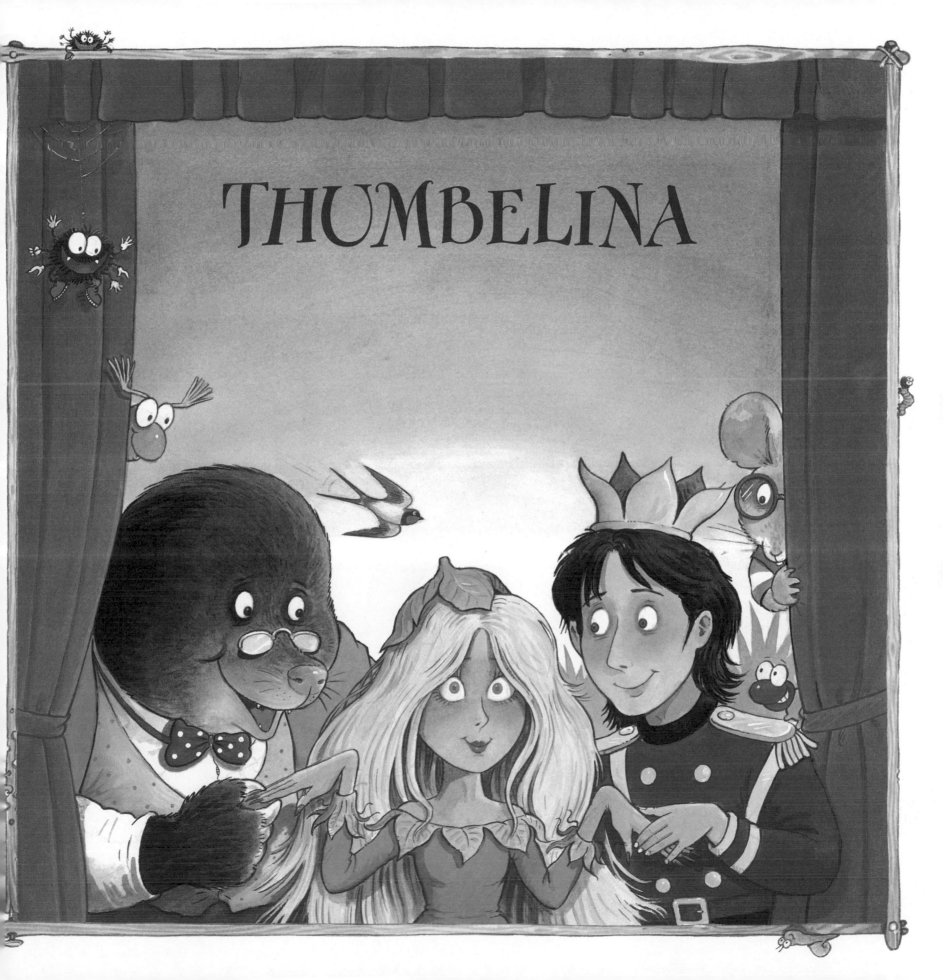

THUMBELINA

Once there was a woman who desperately wanted to have a child. As time passed and she still had no child, she went to visit a witch and asked her for help. To her surprise, the witch gave her a grain of barley. "Take this grain and plant it in a flower pot. Then wait to see what happens," said the witch. "Don't forget to water it well and be patient."

The woman ran home and planted the barley right away.

Every day the woman watered the grain of barley.
Weeks went by and nothing happened. One afternoon,
to the woman's astonishment, a beautiful flower sprang
up out of the pot. In the middle of the flower sat the
tiniest girl the woman had ever seen. She was no larger
than her thumb.

"She's so tiny – I'll call her Thumbelina."
said the woman. She was delighted
to have a child at last and
took great care of her.
Thumbelina was
a cheerful and
contented child.

121

Thumbelina was so tiny that she drank from an acorn cup, and at night, she slept in a walnut shell for a bed.

One night, as Thumbelina lay asleep on the window ledge, an old toad hopped by. Looking through the window, she saw Thumbelina.

"She'll make a nice wife for my son," thought the toad. So she picked Thumbelina up and took her home.

The toad carried Thumbelina down to the stream where she lived. Then she placed Thumbelina on a lily pad, far out in the middle of the stream.

"She can't escape from here," she said to her son. When Thumbelina woke up and saw where she was, she began to cry. The fish in the stream felt sorry for her and cut through the lily stalk. Thumbelina started to float down the stream.

The toad and her son chased after the lily pad. "Come back!" called the son. "You're to be my bride today, Thumbelina!" But just as the toads reached the lily, a beetle swooped down and snatched Thumbelina away.

Thumbelina wondered whatever was to become of her. On and on they travelled, but then the beetle's legs grew tired and eventually he lost his grip on her. Luckily, she landed in the soft leaves of a tree in the forest. There she lived alone all summer. She was happy in the woods, feeding off nuts and berries.

At last the days grew cooler. Winter was setting in and Thumbelina started to feel bitterly cold.

"I must find a shelter," she thought to herself.

Thumbelina set off through the forest to look for a place to shelter for the winter. After walking for several hours, she reached a cornfield, where she stopped to rest.

"You look cold and tired," said a squeaky voice. Thumbelina turned around to see an old mouse.

"Come home with me and have something to eat," he said.

"Oh, thank you!" cried Thumbelina.

The mouse led her down into his cozy home underground. He sat her down before the fire and fed her tea and cakes.

"You can stay here all winter," said the mouse, "if you'll clean and cook for me."

Thumbelina was happy to stay in the mouse's home. He was quite lonely and glad of the company, so they chattered away merrily all day long. Then one day, the mouse introduced Thumbelina to his neighbor, the mole. He was smartly dressed in the finest clothes.

"He is very clever and will make you a fine husband," said the mouse. Soon enough, the mole asked Thumbelina to marry him. She agreed because the mole was a friend of the mouse, who had been so kind to her.

But Thumbelina didn't want to marry the mole. It made her very unhappy to think that she would have to say goodbye to the sun and live underground forevermore.

As soon as Thumbelina agreed to marry the mole, he began to dig a tunnel from his home to the mouse's. The next day, the mole invited Thumbelina to see his house.

Walking through the tunnel, she stumbled across a bird lying across her path. It was a swallow and it was lying very still.

"Don't worry about that dead old bird!" cried the mole grandly, pushing past it. Later, when she made her way home, Thumbelina stopped beside the bird.

"Poor thing!" she cried. "You must have died of cold."

Thumbelina ran to fetch a blanket and spread it over the bird. Then she lay down beside the bird and leaned her head against its feathery breast. To her amazement, she heard a faint *thump! thump!* The swallow's tiny heart was beating! The bird lifted its head and smiled at Thumbelina.

"I was numb with cold and dying," he said, "but you have warmed me and brought me back to life. Thank you."

Every day, Thumbelina took good care of the swallow. She fed and nursed him back to full health.

When spring came and the sun's warmth could be felt underground, the swallow was strong enough to fly home.

"Will you come with me?" he asked. Thumbelina longed to say yes, but instead she shook her head.

"I can't. I've promised to marry the mole," she cried.

"Goodbye then, kind Thumbelina," said the swallow, and flew up into the sunshine and away.

All through the summer, Thumbelina and the mouse were kept busy making preparations for her marriage to the mole. Every day that the mole came to visit her, she liked him less and grew more unhappy.

The day of the wedding arrived, and Thumbelina went into the cornfield to look at the sun one last time before living underground for ever.

"Goodbye, beautiful sun!" she called and started to cry. At that moment she heard a noise.

"Tweet, tweet!"

Looking up into the sky, Thumbelina saw her friend – the swallow!

"Why are you crying?" asked the bird.

"Because I'm going to marry the mole this very day! And then I'll have to live underground for the rest of my life and never see the sun again," sobbed Thumbelina.

"Please don't cry," said the swallow gently. "It's time for me to fly south again, and this time I hope very much that you will agree to come with me."

After a moment's hesitation, Thumbelina climbed onto the swallow's back. Off they flew towards the sun. They flew over fields and woods, over forests and then out across the ocean.

131

Thumbelina felt a warm breeze on her cheek as at last the swallow landed in a garden of flowers, next to a palace.

"This is my home," said the swallow. "You can live here, too. Choose any flower to live in." Thumbelina climbed down onto an orchid. To her surprise, in the middle of it sat a tiny boy with wings, wearing a golden crown.

"Welcome!" he said. "I am the Flower King."

Thumbelina was utterly astonished, for the Flower King was exactly the same size as she was. Then she looked around and saw that all the flowers had tiny people in them, too.

It was love at first sight for Thumbelina and the Flower King. When he asked her to marry him, she readily agreed, and they were married the very next day. After the ceremony, the Flower King gave Thumbelina a tiny pair of wings so that she could fly with him from flower to flower, forever and ever.

And as for the mole? At first, he was inconsolable with grief. "My beautiful bride has gone!" he wept dolefully. The mouse tried to cheer him up with tea and cakes. "You would never have been happy together," said the mouse. "You need the comfort of your cozy underground home, and Thumbelina needs the sun." At last the mole cheered up. "You're right, my friend," he admitted. "I really do prefer my own company."

THE FROG PRINCE

Once there lived a king who had just one daughter. Since she was his only child, she wanted for nothing. She had a wardrobe bursting with fine clothes and a pony to ride. But for all this, the princess was lonely.

"How I wish I had a friend," she sighed. On her birthday, the king gave her a present.

"Happy birthday," he said. "Wow, thanks, Dad," said the princess. It was a beautiful golden ball.

The princess dropped all her other presents and snatched up the golden ball. Then she rushed out into the palace garden. There she played with the ball all day long, throwing it up into the air and catching it.

She was so excited with her father's gift that she threw it higher and higher. All of a sudden, a gust of wind took the ball and lifted it right over the castle walls.

"Whoops," exclaimed the princess. "I hope I haven't lost my precious present. I'd better look for it, before someone else takes it."

The princess dashed out of the castle in time to see the ball flying off towards the forest. She watched as the ball plopped into a pond and sank.

"Oh dear, what shall I do?" she groaned. "I'll never get it back now."

Just then, there was a loud splash and a frog jumped
up on to a lily pad in the middle of the pond.

"Aaarrrgh! Get away from me, you nasty thing!"
screamed the princess. Then, to her astonishment,
the frog spoke to her.

"I'll find your golden ball for you, but first you must
promise to take me home with you and treat
me kindly as a friend," he croaked.

"All right then, Warty,"
said the princess rudely.
She desperately
wanted her
ball back.

The frog dived down to the bottom of the pond and, sure enough, up he came with the golden ball clamped between his clammy fingers. But when he gave the princess her ball, she jumped up and ran off with it!

"Wait," croaked the frog. "Take me with you as you promised you would!"

"Not likely," shouted the princess. "You're far too ugly." And the princess ran home as fast as her legs would carry her. She dashed through the castle gate and slammed it behind her.

"That's the last I'll see of that vile frog, I hope," she muttered to herself.

The princess rushed to tell her father what had happened. "I lost my ball, and to get it back I had to promise a rotten old frog I'd be his friend," she told the king.

"You must keep your promise," said the king.

The princess couldn't believe her ears.

"But it's my birthday!" she cried.
"And he's really ugly and covered in warts."

"You have made a promise and you must keep it," said the king.

At that moment, a croaking noise could be heard coming from outside the castle gate.

"Let me in!" croaked the frog. But the princess just rolled her eyes and crossed her arms.

"You must let the poor fellow in," the king insisted.
Reluctantly, the princess went down to the gate and opened it.
Immediately, the frog hopped up to her and looked her
straight in the eye.

"To show that we are friends," he said, "let me sit beside
you at your party and share your birthday treats."

"I ... um, I'm not sure ..." said the princess.
But before she had finished speaking,
the frog had hopped past
her and was making
his way towards
the dining hall.

143

The princess was very unwilling to let the frog join in her birthday party. "Look here," she whispered. "You can have my finest clothes and even my pony. Just leave me alone."

But the frog replied, "I don't want any of your things. I only want to be your friend."

Reluctantly, the princess let the frog sit beside her at the table, but when she thought the king wasn't looking, she pushed the frog into a bowl of jelly.

"I don't like jelly," croaked the frog. "Let me share the food from your plate."

The princess was about to shake her head, but she saw that the king was frowning at her. Slowly, she pushed her plate over to the frog and was forced to let him share her food. First, the frog tasted a large piece of pizza and then a slice of cake.

"Delicious!" he cried, as he smacked his wet lips with his slimy fingers and slurped his juice through a straw. The princess began to feel quite sick.

Once the frog had eaten his fill, he turned to the birthday
girl again.

"Now, Princess," he said. "It is my dearest wish that
you should kiss me."

"No way!" shrieked the princess. "That's disgusting!"

The frog suddenly leaped up towards her from the table.
The princess clamped her hand over her
mouth to stifle a scream.

"Remember your promise!"
hissed her father. "You must do
what you can to be his friend."

Try as she might, the princess could not persuade her father to take her side. The king was frowning so hard that in the end, she had to agree to kiss the frog, even though it was her birthday.

"I'm only doing this because you made me," she whispered to her father. "I'm not doing it for *him*!"

She closed her eyes as tightly as she possibly could, counted to ten, took a deep breath, puckered up her lips and kissed the frog's damp, warty head.

147

"Open your eyes," said a voice that didn't sound a bit like a frog's. When the princess did open her eyes again, she was utterly amazed to see a devastatingly handsome prince in front of her.

"Who are you?" she gasped.

"I am a prince who was turned into a frog by a wicked witch," he told her. "She said that the spell would only be broken if a princess took me into her castle, shared her food with me, and kissed me. Your kiss has broken the spell. You are the loveliest girl I have ever seen in my life," the prince continued, "and now I would like to marry you."

The princess felt very ashamed for treating the prince so badly when he had been a frog. He looked so kind and friendly and handsome now that he was human.

"All right then," she said. "If Dad doesn't mind, and if you can forgive me for being so rude, I'll marry you."

They rushed to tell the king, who was delighted at the news, and the couple was married with great joy the very next day.

In due course, the princess
and the frog prince had lots
of children, and they all lived
happily ever after.
The children played in the
castle garden every day,
and it came as no surprise
that their favorite game turned
out to be – leapfrog!

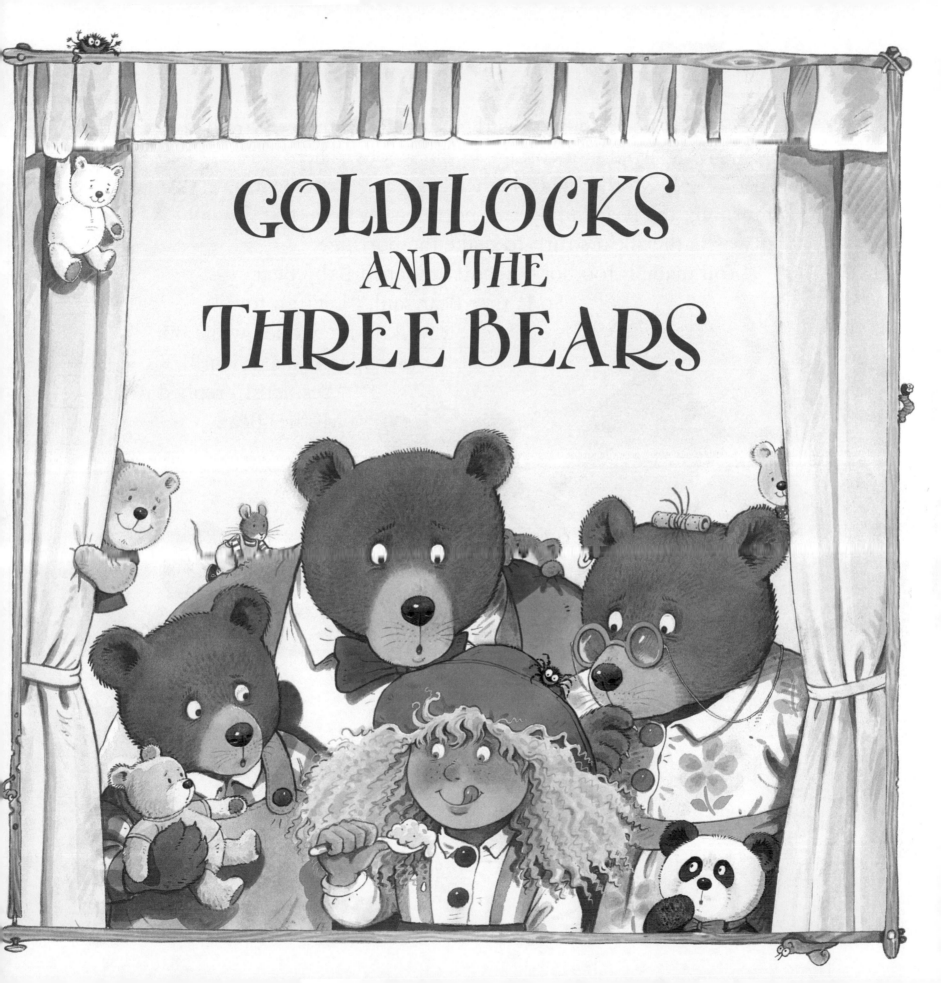

GOLDILOCKS
AND THE
THREE BEARS

nce upon a time there was a family of bears who lived in a cottage in the woods. There was Mother Bear, Father Bear, and Baby Bear. Every morning, the bear family had porridge for breakfast. Today, it was Father Bear's turn to make the porridge.

"You made it too hot – again!" moaned Baby Bear.

So Father Bear said, "Let's go for a walk in the woods while our porridge cools down."

"Yes, let's!" replied Mother Bear.

The bear family set off into the woods while their porridge cooled. A little while later, who should come along the path towards the cottage than a little girl with long golden hair named Goldilocks.

"Oh my!" she said. "What a sweet little cottage. I wonder who lives here." She didn't bother to knock at the door of the cottage. She marched straight in as if she owned the place. She didn't even wipe her muddy feet on the doormat!

Goldilocks was very rude. She saw the three bowls of porridge on the table and she took a taste from each bowl in turn. First, she tasted Father Bear's porridge.

"Yuck! Too salty," she said. Then she tasted Mother Bear's. "How horrid!" she cried. "Too sweet!"

Finally, Goldilocks tried the porridge in Baby Bear's bowl.
It smelled good, it looked good, and Goldilocks couldn't
resist dipping into the bowl with two spoons at once.

"Mmmmm – this isn't either too salty or too sweet.
In fact, it's just right," she mumbled with her mouth full,
which is a very rude thing to do.

Goldilocks ate up every little bit of Baby Bear's
porridge and made a terrible mess.
She spilled the milk and
left great globs of
porridge all over the
tablecloth, too.

After eating,
Goldilocks sat down
in Father Bear's chair.
"This one's too hard,"
she grumbled. Then she
sat in Mother Bear's chair.
"This one's too soft,"
she grumbled again.
"What awful chairs
these are!"

Then Goldilocks spotted Baby Bear's little chair.
"I'll bet this one's just right," she said and flopped into it.
CRASH! Goldilocks was far too big for the chair.
It broke into pieces, and Goldilocks fell onto the floor
with a bump. But naughty Goldilocks just stared at
the bits of wood and muttered,
    "Who cares? I don't!"

Soon Goldilocks began to feel sleepy, so she went upstairs to the bedroom. The naughty girl jumped onto Father Bear's bed – and she still had her muddy shoes on!

"This bed is far too bouncy!" she shrieked. And then she had a wonderful time bouncing up and down on Father Bear's bed, as if it were a trampoline.

Then she tried out Mother Bear's middle-sized bed.

"This bed's far too soft!" she said, sinking down on the pillows – with her muddy shoes on!

Goldilocks looked around. There must be another bed, surely? Then she spotted the tiniest bed of all. It belonged to Baby Bear, of course. It was the loveliest, most inviting looking bed that Goldilocks had ever seen. It was shaped like a baby bear and covered in a comfy patchwork quilt.

Goldilocks swept all of Baby Bear's toys off his bed onto the floor and then she jumped into it, clothes, muddy shoes and all!

"This is lovely," she said sleepily. "Oh, dear, I do feel rather tired...." Goldilocks was so full of nice, warm porridge and so exhausted from jumping on the bears' chairs and beds, that in the wink of an eye she was fast asleep and soon snoring gently!

A little while later, the bears
returned from their walk eager for their
breakfast. They opened the door and could
not believe their eyes. There was porridge
everywhere!

"What a state!" cried Father Bear.

"Good heavens!" cried Mother Bear.

"Who made this big mess?" said Baby Bear.

They looked at the bowls of porridge on the table and stared in disbelief.

"Someone's been eating my porridge," said Father Bear, looking at the horrid mess around his bowl.

"Someone's been eating my porridge, too," said Mother Bear, looking at the mess around her bowl.

"Well, someone's been eating my porridge, too," said Baby Bear, who was starting to cry. "And they've eaten up every last drop!"

It was true. The three bears stared at Baby Bear's bowl and shook their heads. Not only was his porridge gone, but the bowl had been licked clean!

Then they saw the chairs.
"Someone's been sitting in my chair," said Father Bear.
"Someone's been sitting in my chair, too!" said Mother Bear.
"Someone's been sitting in my chair and broken it!" cried Baby Bear.

"We'd better take a look upstairs," said Father Bear.
"Who knows what we'll find there!" The three bears
cautiously climbed the stairs. Then they slowly opened
the bedroom door. What they saw filled them with dismay.
   "Someone's been sleeping in my bed," exclaimed Father
Bear, as he looked at the broken bedsprings and his clothes
all scattered everywhere.

   "Someone's been sleeping in my bed,
   too!" said Mother Bear, as she looked
   at the dent in the pillows.
      "Someone's been sleeping in my
      bed," squealed Baby Bear, pointing
      at Goldilocks' tousled locks,
      "and she's still there!"

The bears' loud voices woke Goldilocks from her slumbers. At first she opened one eye and murmured, "Mmmm ... lovely, comfy bed ..." Then she sat bolt upright and stifled a scream. There were three bears standing around the bed, and they looked very surprised indeed! At first, she pulled the quilt up over her head and hoped that the bears would not eat her up. Then suddenly, she felt very ashamed of all the mess and trouble that she had caused.

"Oh dear," she sniffed, as she lifted the quilt off her face again. "I ... I ... I ... am so t-t-terribly sorry. I didn't mean any harm."

Luckily, the bears were very kind, and soon they saw the funny side of it, too. "I'm glad my porridge was too salty for you to eat!" chortled Father Bear.

"And I'm glad mine was too sweet!" laughed Mother Bear, wiping a tear from her eye.

Goldilocks helped tidy up the cottage. Then Father Bear made a fresh pot of porridge.

"This porridge is just right," said Goldilocks politely.

After Goldilocks had eaten her fill of
the delicious porridge, she said a fond
farewell to the three bears and skipped
back through the woods to her home.
Her mother and father were waiting
anxiously at the door for her.
"Where have you been?" they demanded.
"Oh, I got into a mess, but I'm all
right now!" replied Goldilocks. "I don't
want any breakfast, though," she added.

PUSS-IN-BOOTS

Once upon a time there was a miller who had three sons. When he died, all that he left to his three sons was his mill, his donkey, and his cat. The eldest son took the mill while the second son took the donkey.

The youngest son was left with just the cat, whose job it was to chase the mice that made holes in the sacks of flour to steal the grain.

"Poor Puss won't be much use to me," the young lad sighed. "I can't make money out of dead mice. I shall just have to go out into the world to seek my fortune."

168

"Don't worry. I can help you," said Puss to his new master. "If you will give me a pair of fine boots and a drawstring sack, I promise you that one day, you will be richer than either of your brothers."

The youngest son was so astonished to hear the cat speak that he did exactly as he was told. He hurried off without a word and soon returned with a drawstring sack and a handsome pair of the finest leather boots. Puss was pleased with what he saw. He immediately pulled the leather boots onto his hind paws, and found they fit him purrrfectly!

Wearing his fine new boots and with the sack slung over his shoulder, Puss strode proudly out into the fields without so much as a backward glance. He headed for a rabbit warren, where he opened the sack wide and laid it next to the hole. Then he put some carrots inside the sack.

Puss lay down behind the sack and waited until two rabbits came by. They hopped inside the sack to eat the carrots. Up sprang Puss, who pulled the drawstring tight and set off for the palace.

"Your Majesty," said Puss, taking a low bow, "my master, the Marquis of Carabas, was out hunting today and was lucky enough to catch a pair of wild rabbits. He begs you to accept them as a gift." (The Marquis of Carabas was the name Puss had made up for his new master.) The king was truly delighted.

"Hooray, I love rabbit stew!" he cried. "Please thank the Marquis of Carabas very much for his fine present."

The next day, Puss went out into the fields again. This time he took a handful of grain from the mill and caught two wild pheasants in his sack. Right away he was off to the palace to present his catch to the king again.

"Hooray! I love roast pheasant," cried the king. "The Marquis of Carabas must be a generous and noble man."

Puss carried on like this day after day. Soon he began to hear all the court gossip, until one day he found out that the king was planning an outing in his carriage.

By the next morning, Puss had hatched a great plan.

"The king will be driving past the river at noon with his beautiful daughter," he told his master. "Go and bathe in the river and leave everything to me." The Marquis of Carabas nodded. He had no idea what Puss was talking about, but he trusted the cat to keep his word about making his fortune.

As midday approached, the young lad plunged into the river. It was icy cold and his teeth chattered. Meanwhile, Puss hid his master's ragged clothes under a stone and waited for the king's carriage to pass.

At noon, just as the king was passing by the river in his carriage, Puss began to shout, "Help! Help! The Marquis of Carabas has been robbed!" The king looked out of the carriage window to see the lad in the river. He at once wanted to help the marquis who had sent him such kind gifts.

"Stop!" yelled the king to his carriage driver. The driver pulled on the pony's reins, and the animal skidded to a halt.

The king leaped out of the carriage and ran to the river.

"Wretched thieves stole my master's clothes while he was bathing," cried Puss. "He cannot appear before your daughter without any clothes!"

"Of course not," said the king and sent the driver to fetch a spare set of clothes from the back of the carriage.

"Give these to your master and tell him I'll give him a lift home in the carriage, poor chap," the king said to crafty Puss.

The king got back inside the carriage and drew the curtain closed, while Puss dressed his master in the beautiful clothes. Puss watched as the marquis stepped into the carriage.

The King went to shake his hand, but the marquis' eyes were on the princess. The princess swooned.

"I knew the marquis was rich, but he's so handsome, too!" she thought.

Once he had made sure that the marquis was happily installed in the king's carriage, Puss raced off to talk to some men working in the fields.

"When the king drives past, tell him all the land for miles around belongs to the Marquis of Carabas," ordered Puss. "Or I will have your heads cut off!"

Now Puss knew that the field belonged to an ogre who was able to change his shape. The poor men didn't know if Puss was just a cat – or the ogre in disguise – so they did as Puss told them.

Puss sped off again until he came to a huge castle. The ogre lived there, and Puss had a plan. Bold as anything, he marched straight up to the castle door and asked to speak to the ogre.

"Ogre," said Puss, "I've heard you can turn yourself into an elephant. But I can't believe it's true!" The ogre was so offended that he grunted, "OH YES I CAN!" and at once turned into an elephant.

"That's amazing! You truly frightened me," said Puss. "But can you turn yourself into something as small as, say, a mouse?"

The foolish ogre grunted again and turned himself into a tiny mouse. Quick as a flash, Puss pounced upon the mouse and gobbled him up bones, tail, and all.

A few minutes later, Puss heard the king's carriage arriving at the castle door.

"Welcome to the home of the Marquis of Carabas," Puss announced with a flourish, as he ushered in the king and his daughter.

"My goodness, you are a rich chap," said the king to the lad. "You send me gifts, you own all the land for miles around, and this is your castle, too!"

But the marquis said nothing at all. In fact he wasn't even listening to the king.

The Marquis of Carabas was busy gazing intently into the princess's eyes. It was obvious to the king that the pair of them were falling in love.

"You're rich and you like her, so I suppose you can marry her if you like," he sighed contentedly.

"Hooray!" cried the marquis.

"I'll say!" the princess joined in cheerfully.

And so they were married that very day and lived happily ever after, all thanks to Puss-in-Boots.

And as for Puss-in-Boots,
his master was so grateful that
he saw to it that the cat was made a lord.
Puss never had to chase a mouse
ever again. Indeed, he lived the rest
of his life in great comfort,
style, and luxury.

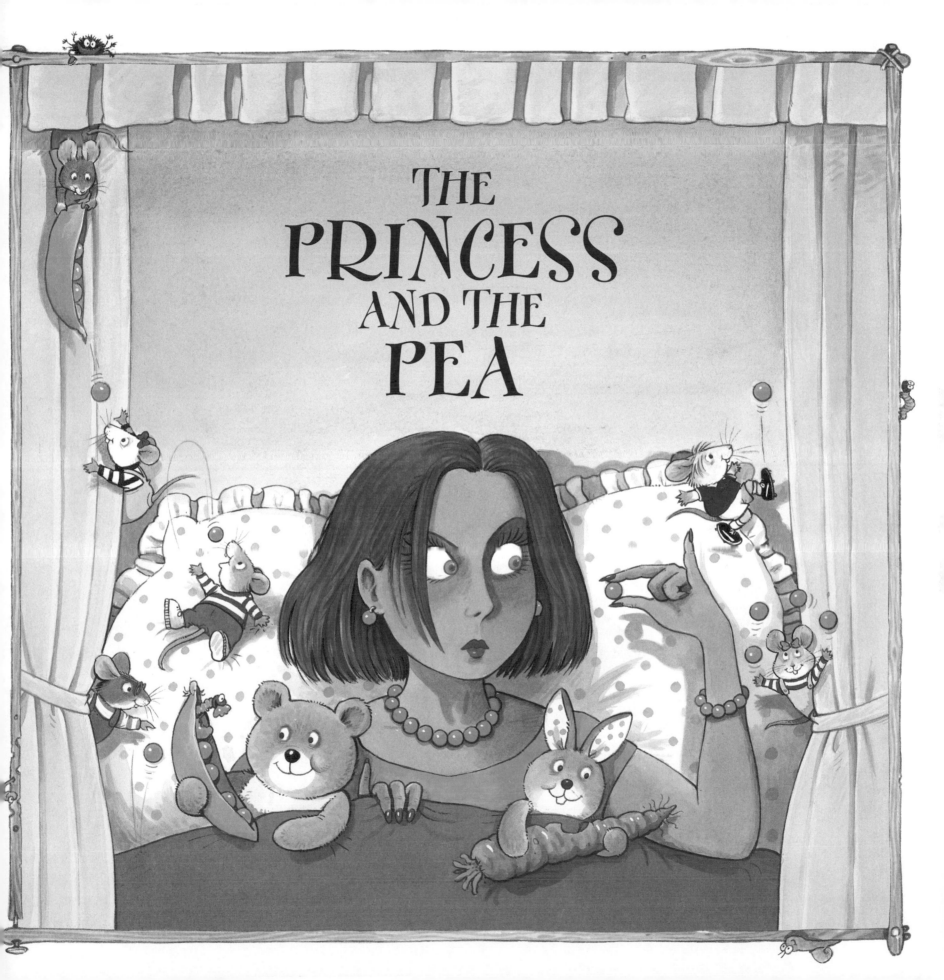

THE PRINCESS AND THE PEA

here once was a young prince who wanted to marry. He had travelled all over the world in search of his queen and still he was alone. Maybe he was extremely fussy, but it wasn't an easy task! And besides, how was he to know if all the girls who said they were princesses really were princesses?

"There are tall girls and short ones, intelligent ones and dumb ones, funny princesses and sad ones, and even musical ones," sighed the prince, who sometimes felt dizzy with all the choice he had. "They all claim to be genuinely royal – but perhaps they're all fakes!"

However, there was more to it than that. With every princess he met, he knew there was something important missing.

"Not one of them has *all* the qualities that I am searching for and I don't love any of them!" he thought. As the cast of yet another show lined up to greet him, he felt frustrated and too tired to travel any more.

"I'm going home!" he declared. "I shall enjoy my own company instead. Besides, I miss my mom and dad – not to mention my teddy bear!"

Back at home, the prince soon felt lonely again. He decided to join a date-a-princess agency. He was on the point of choosing a princess to meet from the agency catalogue when there was an unexpected knock at the door.

Warily he opened the door,
to find a very beautiful
girl sitting on a motorbike
right outside.

The girl smiled sweetly
and then she explained,
"I'm a princess who
has lost my way.
Is there any chance
of staying for a night,
please?"

The prince was
delighted by this
unusual princess
and he immediately
invited her inside.

"Come and meet my parents," said the prince. "They'll love you." For he had already fallen in love with her at first sight.

However, the queen was not so happy about the princess. She thought, "This messy, bike-riding young girl could never be a princess!" She didn't like the idea of her royal son spending time with her. "She's an unsuitable companion for the heir to the throne," she whispered to the king.

The queen was very clever and she thought of a plan to test whether this girl was a real princess.

"Welcome, my dear," she said sweetly to her. "You look tired, so I'm sure you'd like an early night. Please wait here while we make a bed ready for you."

Then the queen made the king and the prince prepare a bed of twenty mattresses for the girl to sleep on. At the very bottom, right in the middle, the queen placed one very tiny dried-up pea. "Now we'll see!" she said to herself.

The girl was tired indeed.

"How kind of the queen to go out of her way to make me comfortable," she thought. "All those mattresses look beautifully cozy." She snuggled down under the quilt, but unfortunately she just couldn't get comfortable. She wriggled, tossed, and turned, but nothing worked!

"Ouch!" she cried out. There was a hard bump in the bed that felt like a mountain. "Whatever can it be?" the wretched girl thought. She looked under the first mattress but there was nothing there. Of course, she didn't think of looking under the twentieth mattress...

Soon the girl gave up trying to sleep. She lay awake all night thinking of the young prince, instead.

In the morning the girl made her way down the spiral staircase. Not only did the stairs creak, but it felt as though every bone in her body creaked as well! The king, queen, and prince were happily eating a breakfast feast at their banqueting table.

"Did you sleep well?" the queen enquired.

"Oh, yes, thank you," the girl replied, not wishing to appear ungrateful. "Have some breakfast!" said the queen.

"Thank you," said the girl, stifling a yawn.

She sat down at the end of the table, and the royal family resumed their feasting. The king looked up.

"What's that noise?" he said. The family looked down the table to where the poor girl had fallen asleep over her breakfast and was snoring gently. The king was most distressed and immediately asked,

"What's the matter?"

"Something hard was in my bed," the girl admitted, "and now I feel battered black and blue. I didn't have a wink of sleep, to tell you the truth."

To everyone's great surprise, the queen suddenly burst out into rapturous applause.

"She's a real princess!" she cried happily. "Only a real princess could possibly feel one tiny pea underneath twenty mattresses. Congratulations, my dear!"

"Hooray!" cried the prince, who had – not very secretly – been admiring her all along! And so saying, he slid the entire length of the banqueting table to be at the princess's side.

He came skidding to a halt in front of her. The princess grinned shyly as he lay on the banqueting table and gazed intently into her eyes, with love in his heart. Luckily, she, too, was falling in love with him.

The queen realized that this girl had ALL the qualities of a true princess.

"I think she is a suitable companion for the heir to the throne, after all," she whispered to the king, as they tiptoed out of the banqueting hall.

"I agree with you!" replied the king.

The prince and princess were now deeply in love with each other, and so it really was quite lucky that she was a real princess.

The prince said, "If I promise never to put a pea, bean, or any other vegetable in your bed, will you marry me?"

"There's nothing I'd like better," she said. Then they went for a spin on her motorbike, so that the prince could show her around the palace grounds and the rest of the royal family's land.

They enjoyed themselves so much that they travelled around the kingdom for a year and a day. Then they were married in great style and had a wonderful feast with all kinds of delicious things to eat – but absolutely, positively NO peas!

They lived together happily and eventually, when the old king died, they became king and queen.

Even though they were now
king and queen, they continued
to drive around the kingdom on her
motorbike. In fact, nothing much
changed – except for one thing.
The new queen sent out an order:
"All peas in the kingdom are
to be banned, forever."
And they were!

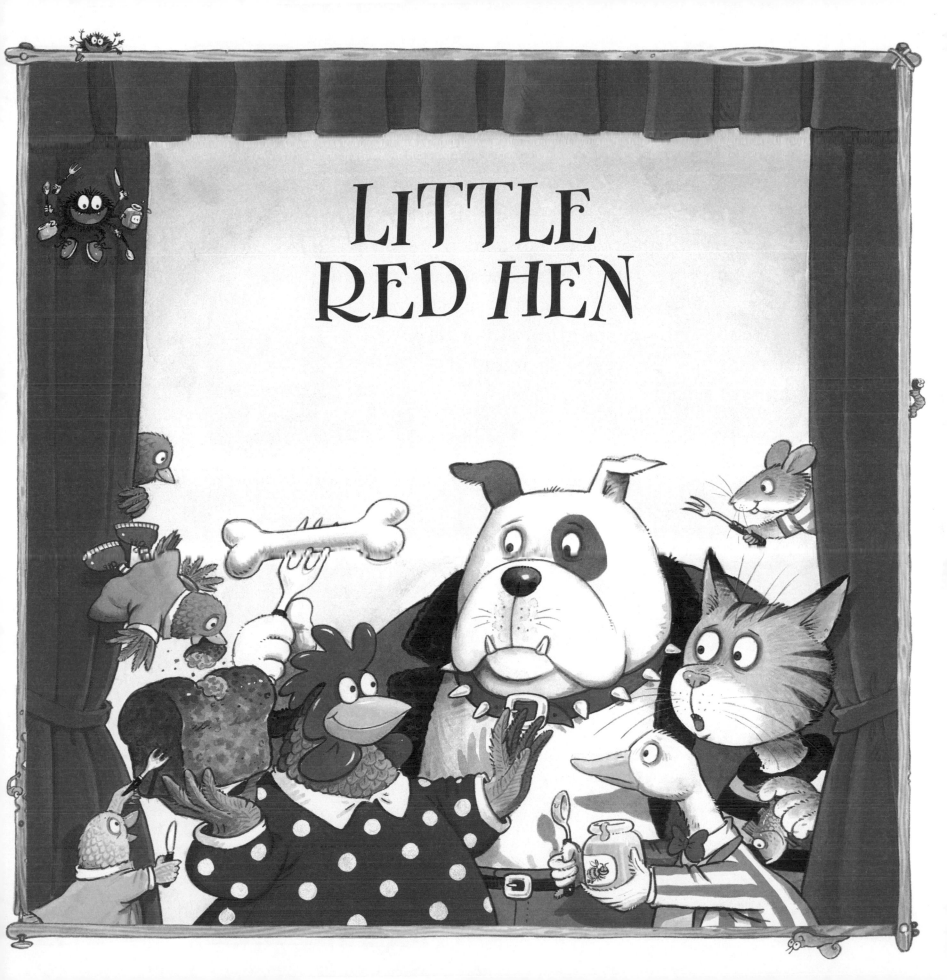

LITTLE RED HEN

Once upon a time, there lived a little red hen. She lived on a farm with her chicks and her friends the duck, the cat, and the dog. Every day, the little red hen scratched in the farmyard, looking for seeds and worms to feed her chicks.

One morning, the little red hen was scratching as usual, when all of a sudden, she stopped and looked intently at the ground. For there beneath her very eyes was a golden grain of wheat.

"Now here's something special," said the little red hen to herself. "If I plant this grain of wheat, then it will grow and produce more grains of wheat. And then we'll all have plenty of delicious bread to eat." She felt so excited that she was determined to plant the grain of wheat straight away. She decided to ask her friends the duck, the cat, and the dog to help her. "Which one of you will help me plant this grain of wheat?" she asked them.

But the little red hen's friends were too tired and lazy
to be bothered to help her.
"I won't help you!" said the duck, dozing off.
"Nor I!" said the cat, yawning.
"Nor I!" said the dog,
stretching his legs.
"Then my chicks and I will
have to plant the grain of wheat
by ourselves," said the
little red hen.

So the little red hen and her chicks planted the grain of wheat. They dug the ground and raked it. Then they made a hole and popped the grain in and gave it some water. Finally one day, a green shoot appeared above the earth. Soon the shoot grew into a tall stalk of green wheat.

Then the wheat began to ripen. Gradually it turned golden yellow and at last it was ready to be cut.

"Who will help me and my chicks to cut the wheat?" said the little red hen.

"I won't," said the duck, and he dived into the pond.

"I won't either," said the cat, as he ran into the house.

"Nor I," said the dog, as he gnawed at a bone.

So the little red hen and her chicks cut the wheat down all by themselves. It was hard work, and when they had finished, they were exhausted.

Now that the wheat had been cut, it was ready to be threshed to separate the grains from the husks. The little red hen went to visit her friends again. She did so hope that they would help her with the threshing.

"Which one of you will help me and my chicks to thresh the wheat?" she said. "Will it be you, duck, or you, cat, or will it even be dog?"

There was a silence in the farmyard. The friends looked at their feet. Then they all spoke at once.

"Not I, I've got things to do," said the duck, as he pulled a worm from the ground.

"Nor I, I'm busy," said the cat, as he chased a mouse.

"Me neither," said the dog, who wasn't doing anything.

So the little red hen and her chicks had to thresh the wheat all by themselves.

Now the wheat was ready to be taken to the mill to be ground into flour.

"Which one of you will help my chicks and me to take this wheat to the mill?" said the little red hen.

"I'm sorry, I'm going fishing," said the duck, as he lay back in his boat and idly cast a line over the side.

"Oh!" said the little red hen, and went to ask the cat.

"I'm sorry. It's far too cold. I'm staying warm and dry by the fire," said the cat.

"And I've got to keep guard over the house," said the dog, sitting down on the doorstep.

"Oh well," said the little red hen, "I'll manage." So she and her chicks dragged the wheat to the mill. When the wheat had been ground into flour, it was ready to be made into bread.

"Who will help me make this flour into bread?" said the little red hen.

"Not I," said the lazy duck.

"Nor I!" said the lazy cat.

"Me neither!" said the lazy dog.

"Never mind," said the little red hen. "I somehow thought I couldn't rely on any of you."

So she and her chicks poured the soft white flour into a big bowl. They added water and yeast to the flour and stirred it and kneaded it until it had turned into dough. Then they put the dough in the oven.

When it was baked, they took the bread out of the oven, and it smelled wonderful.

"Mmmm!" said the chicks. The delicious smell of the bread wafted out into the farmyard.

The duck, the cat, and the dog sniffed the air and followed their noses to the kitchen window. The bread was ready to be eaten.

"Which of you will help me eat this bread?" said the little red hen, as she carried the bread to the table.

"I will!" said the duck, hastily.

"Me too!" said the cat, greedily.

"And me!" said the dog, rudely.

"Oh no, you won't!" said the little red hen. "You wouldn't help my chicks and me to plant the grain, or cut it, or thresh it. And you wouldn't help me to take the wheat to the mill, or bake the bread. My chicks and I are going to eat the bread – every last crumb!"

The three friends could only look astonished as the little red hen slammed the window in their faces.

The little red hen cut the bread into thick slices. Then she buttered each slice of bread with thick slabs of yellow butter. She gave the slices to her chicks and kept the crust for herself. They ate up every last crumb. And it was the very best bread that they had ever eaten!

They felt very full indeed. But it was worth it just to see the envious faces of the lazy duck, the lazy cat, and the lazy dog.

"Next time I find a grain of wheat," chuckled the little red hen, "maybe you'll help me!"

THE END

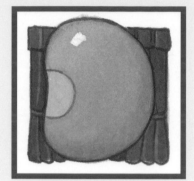

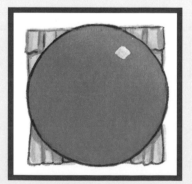